Kai Lüftner was born in East Berlin. An author of books for children and young adults, he is also a musician, audiobook editor, and director. Over the course of his career he has published more than twenty books, while his children's music project Rotz 'n' Roll has enjoyed great success and played lots of concerts. Lüftner lives with his family on the Danish island of Bornholm in the Baltic Sea.

Wiebke Rauers was born in Düsseldorf, where she studied communication design with a concentration in illustration. After receiving her degree she moved to Berlin and worked as a character designer in an animation studio. Since 2015 she has worked as a freelance illustrator of children's books; she has also done illustration work for film and television. She lives in Berlin with her daughter, husband, and lots of stuffed animals.

Text copyright © 2022 by Kai Lüftner.
Illustrations copyright © 2022 by Wiebke Rauers.
First published in Switzerland under the title *Marie Käferchen*.

English translation copyright © 2023 by NorthSouth Books, Inc., New York 10016.
Translated by Marshall Yarbrough.
All rights reserved. No part of this book may be reproduced or utilized in any form or by any means, electronic or mechanical, including photocopying, recording, or any information storage and retrieval system, without permission in writing from the publisher.
First published in the United States, Great Britain, Canada, Australia, and New Zealand in 2023 by NorthSouth Books, Inc., an imprint of NordSüd Verlag AG, CH-8050 Zürich, Switzerland.
Distributed in the United States by NorthSouth Books, Inc., New York 10016. Library of Congress Cataloging-in-Publication Data is available.
ISBN: 978-0-7358-4499-5 (trade edition)
1 3 5 7 9 • 10 8 6 4 2
Printed in Latvia
www.northsouth.com

JITTERBUG

Kai Lüftner   Wiebke Rauers

Translated from German
by Marshall Yarbrough

North South

Ladybugs are oh so sweet,
Cutesy, charming, quite petite.

Fluttering from flower to flower,
Resting in a leafy bower,
Gentle, with a bit of whimsy—
Spotted wings—a little flimsy.

Dewdrops glisten on the grass,
Ladybugs hum gaily past,
Never loud or coarse or wild,
Always peaceful, always mild.

But wait—oh my, this can't be good.
What's that thrashing in the wood?
Have you seen this thing before?
Is it . . . rhino? Or wild boar?

Wailing, flailing, little head banging,
Legs hooked over a tree limb, hanging,
Fist raised high—up above the ground,
Baring her teeth and gettin' down.

Not sure you could call it dancing,
Running around, thrashing, strutting–prancing?
Flying, dropping through the air–
On her face a real mean glare.
Who is this creature tearing up the rug?
It's . . . Lady B. Marie . . .

The Jitterbug!

She was always a little . . . or actually, no,
She was always a LOT, from the very get-go.
"Different." Yes, that word's correct—
Not your usual insect.

Papa groans when he hears the noise.
How come she just can't play with toys?
Screeching in her tender years,
Loud punk rock could hurt her ears!

And Papa, he isn't the only one—
The noise complaints have just begun.
Jitterbug tries bold effects—
The forest fills with mad insects.

"Completely inappropriate!"
Ms. Snail finds some fault with it.
Her face is set in pure dismay.
Things didn't used to be this way!

And Mr. Grasshopper chirps, "Agreed!"
This noise is out of line indeed.
He turns his head and tries to go.
Jitterbug shouts: "Enjoy the show!"

Here comes the bass line, rumbling low,
The meadow grass shakes to and fro.
And *pop! bang! crash!* the drums charge in—
And everywhere, frozen in chagrin,
Are creatures who can't believe what they're hearing—
Now here's a guitar solo, red hot, searing!

And Jitterbug, our fearless flyer,
Cranks the volume a few clicks higher,
Growls and grunts with total abandon—
Showing no sign of needing a stand-in.

Pretty soon she was the only one
On the meadow—not yet done.
Her shouting was the only sound,
O'er hill and dale for miles around.

But rather than let herself feel sad,
She ripped a solo—look out, Dad!
She didn't need a herd or a flock.
All she wanted was to rock!
Her voice in the stillness of the wood.
Bearing witness. It felt good!
This was more than glitz and glam.
It was a declaration: "Here I am!"

Rock 'n' roll was her true-blue friend.
And only every now and then
Did Jitterbug long for company,
A friend to help sing harmony.
But whenever she felt this somber notion,
She sang a ballad full of emotion,
And that was the perfect remedy:
turned sadness into melody.

Days passed by—it'd been two weeks.
Jitterbug honed her technique,
Singing, strumming, so athletic,
Regimented—quite kinetic.

Then one day a band of bugs—
You might have recognized their mugs—
Just happened to roll by this way,
Searching for a place to play.

They thought they might have found the spot,
A decent pad, a place to squat.
Practice in a quiet clearing—
But wait, what's this they're hearing?
Wild chords, high-speed melody—
Who else but Lady B. Marie!

There she sat up on her branch,
Roaring like an avalanche,
Like a hailstorm, like a squall,
Belting it out, giving it her all.

The band all gave a little shrug—
Like, hey, there's something to this bug—
And started playing, *ram-tam-tam*,
A heavy, funky punk rock jam,
Wild and free but in control,
A blast of perfect rock 'n' roll!

And soaring high above the ground,
Surfing on the wave of sound,
Right where she was supposed to be—
was Jitterbug—Lady B. Marie.

Then they got to it, and bit by bit
They first had a song and then a hit.
The lean woods were all abuzz
With rumbling bass and guitar fuzz.

Summoned back by the soulful sound,
Mr. Grasshopper pogoed up and down,
Dancing to each decibel.

Ms. Snail came out of her shell.
And everyone else in the wood beside
Came to see Jitterbug—loud and amplified. . . .

And ever since then no one ever cries foul
Whenever the band starts to rock and howl.
When the bass and guitars all start blaring—
The groove's so good they're all past caring.
And when the famous Jitterbug
Starts grunting and growling her melody—
Or making noise, as some admit—
No one has a beef with it.

It might sound like noise to those walking away,
To the people who don't want to sit down and stay.
They refuse to listen and soon say "let's split."
Which is simply to say they just don't get it!

So next time you hear someone grumble or groan,
Ask them to try making noise of their own.
And don't be surprised if they soon see fit
To call what was once "noise" a hit!